Hiccups

by David W. Ball

Dedicated to my amazing son Evan

ISBN 978-1-312-42580-4

**Is it a Hiccup,
Or a Hick-down?
Either way,
It causes a frown.**

Is a Hiccup good?
Is a Hiccup bad?
Do you get them from Mom?
Do you get them from Dad?

**Are Hiccups the same,
Every time?
Are your Hiccups,
The same as mine?**

Why do they start?
Does anybody know?
How do they stop?
Where do they go?

**You can hold your breath,
or ask for a scare...**

If they don't go away it's because, Hiccups aren't fair.

To get rid of your Hiccups,
Just keep this in mind,
They go away on their own,
It just takes some time.

CPSIA information can be obtained
at www.ICGtesting.com
Printed in the USA
LVRC012156100720
660191LV00002B/9

9 781312 425804